-ed ending

A Fish Tale

by J.S. Davis • Illustrated by Rebecca Thornburgh

SCHOLASTIC INC.
New York Toronto London Auckland Sydney

We had fished all morning.
My dad did great, but not me.
You could tell if you looked in my pail.
I had only reeled in one fish.

"Let's grill these fish for lunch," my dad said.
He went off to the car.
He lifted out a small grill.
I looked in my pail again.
One fish. One little, little fish.

3

"This fish is so small," I said.
"Why keep it?" I added.

"Why indeed?" a little voice called out.
"Be kind! Toss me back in."

I looked at my dad.
He did not look back.

"Be kind, toss me back!
Just try it!"
There it was again!
I looked at Dad.
His lips were still.

5

"Who said that?" I asked.
"Down here!" the voice called.
It came from my pail.

I looked down.
"Hi!" said the little fish.

I jumped up.
A fish that talked?
This could not be.
It had to be the sun.
I must be too hot.

"Are you OK?" the fish asked.
"You look hot."
I looked down at the fish.
It smiled and winked at me.
What can you say to a fish?
"I *am* hot," I said.

"Me, too," said the fish.
"Could we move
under the tree?" it asked.
I picked up the pail.
We moved to the shade.
"A talking fish! This is like a
fairy tale," I said.
"More like a fish tale," said the fish.

9

"So what's it like to be a fish?" I asked.
"You swim. You eat. You try not
to get eaten," said the fish.

"I like to swim," I said.
"I like to eat, too."

The fish jumped.

"What do you like to eat?" it said.

"I like to eat all kinds of fff. . ."

"Stop!" said the fish. "Let's make a deal.
I will give you a wish if you toss me back."

". . . food," I said.

"You tricked me!" said the fish.

"Look," I said.

"I do not want you washed and grilled.

I do not want you to stay for lunch.

I do not want you to *be* lunch."

Then I told the fish what I wanted.

"OK," said the fish.
"Toss me back.
You will get your wish."
I got up off the log and went
back to the lake.
I tossed the fish in.

"Good-bye!" I called.
"So long!" the fish
yelled back.

13

My dad came up next to me.

"Did I hear that fish talk?" he asked.

"What?" I asked.

"You must be too hot.
It must be
the sun."

My dad looked up at the sun.
"It *is* hot," he said, "too hot to cook."
"Let's go get ice cream."
"Great!" I said.

I waved. The fish winked.
And that is the end of my fish tale!

Phonics Reader 24 ★ Words to Sound Out

/t/ed	/d/ed	/ed/ed
asked	called	added
fished	grilled	wanted
jumped	reeled	
looked	winked	
picked	yelled	
tossed		
tricked		
washed		

Phonics Reader 24 ★ Words to Remember

again kind(s) move(d) off try

Phonics Reader 24 ★ Story Words

fairy food never talk(ed) voice

16